First published in Great Britain by HarperCollins Publishers Ltd in 1996.
ISBN 0 00 761362 8   Text and illustrations copyright © Ian Beck 1996

POPPY AND PIP'S BEDTIME

Ian Beck

Collins

An Imprint of HarperCollinsPublishers

The moon was high in the sky.
It was Poppy and Pip's bedtime.

"Let's get ready," said Poppy.

Poppy changed into her pyjamas.
Pip checked that all was well.

Poppy brushed her teeth and Pip
shook his coat.
"Into bed, Pip,"
said Poppy.
"Wooof," yawned Pip.
Off went the light.

"Woof, woof, woof!"
On went the light.

"What is it, Pip?" said Poppy.
Pip had lost his toy.

They looked everywhere for
Pip's toy. In the cupboard...
In the toy box...

In the dresser...
And behind the door.

"Not here, Pip," said Poppy.
"Grrooof," said Pip.

Tap. Tap. Tap.

"Who's at the door?" said Poppy.
"Quack!" said a voice.
The little duck had lost her toy.

Poppy, Pip and the little duck
started to hunt for the lost toys.

Scratch. Scratch. Scratch.

"Who's at the door?" said Poppy.
"Miaow!" said a voice.
The little kitten had lost his toy.

Poppy, Pip, the duck and the kitten started to hunt for all the toys.

"Quaaack!" said the little duck.

She had found the kitten's toy.

"Miaow, thank you,"
said the little kitten.

"Miaooww!"
said the little kitten.

He had found the little duck's toy.

"Quack, thank you,"
said the little duck.

"Woooof," said Pip sadly.
"Never mind Pip," said
Poppy, "you can have
my toy tonight."

But when she went to
fetch her toy, she
found Pip's
teddy under
her pillow!

Now everyone was happy.
"Come on," said Poppy, "it's time
you all went home to bed."

Goodnight, sleep tight.